SLIMY SCIENCE

CRUNCHY SLIME

BY

LOUISE NELSON

WINDMILL BOOKS™

Published in 2022 by Windmill Books,
an Imprint of Rosen Publishing
29 East 21st Street, New York, NY 10010

Edited by: Madeline Tyler
Illustrated by: Danielle Rippengill

Cataloging-in-Publication Data

Names: Nelson, Louise.
Title: Crunchy slime / Louise Nelson.
Description: New York : Windmill, 2022. | Series: Slimy science | Includes glossary and index.
Identifiers: ISBN 9781499489491 (pbk.) | ISBN 9781499489514 (library bound) | ISBN 9781499489507 (6pack) | ISBN 9781499489521 (ebook)
Subjects: LCSH: Gums and resins, Synthetic--Juvenile literature. | Handicraft--Juvenile literature.
Classification: LCC TP978.N45 2022 | DDC 620.1'924--dc23

Printed in the United States of America

CPSIA Compliance Information: Batch CWWM22: For Further Information contact Rosen Publishing, New York, New York at 1-800-237-9932

SAFETY AND RESPONSIBILITY INFO FOR GROWN-UPS

Any ingredients used could cause irritation, so don't play with slime for too long, don't put it near your face, and keep it away from babies and young children.

Always wash your hands before and after making slime. Choose kid-safe glues and non-toxic ingredients, and always make sure there is an adult present.

Don't substitute ingredients—we cannot guarantee the results.

Leftover slime can be stored for one more use for up to a week in a sealed container and out of the reach of children. For hygiene reasons, we do not recommend storing slime that has been used in a classroom environment.

Slime is not safe for pets.

Wear a mask around powdered ingredients and goggles around liquid ingredients. Before throwing your slime away, cut it into lots of small pieces. Don't put slime down the drain—always put it in the trash.

GLITTER SLIME!

IMAGE CREDITS: All images are courtesy of Shutterstock.com, unless otherwise specified. With thanks to Getty Images, Thinkstock Photo and iStockphoto. Cover – Zhe Vasylieva, balabolka, Dado Photos, xnova, Lithiumphoto, MAKOVSKY ART, jarabee123, Kuzina Natali. Images used on every page: Heading Font – Zhe Vasylieva. Background – Lithiumphoto. Grid – xnova. Splats – Sonechko57. 2 – Purple Clouds. 4 – jarabee123. 5 – Purple Clouds, AlonaPhoto, Dado Photos. 6 – Tidewater Teddy. 7 – New Africa. 8 – FotoDuets, JanHetman, Veja. 10 – Cipariss, Photo Win1. 11 – AlonaPhoto, KlavdiyaV. 12 – AlonaPhoto. 13 – GO_, photka, timquo, jarabee123. 14 – Alina Demidenko. 15&16 – KlavdiyaV. 17&18 – AbriEl. 19 – Candle photo. 20 – Baby bird818. 20&21 – FamStudio. 21 – Purple Clouds, New Africa. 23 – All for you friend, AnnyStudio, Floral Deco, Good luck images, Handatko, Prezoom.nl.

CONTENTS

Words that look like this can be found in the glossary on page 24.

IT'S SLIME TIME!

Squish it, pull it, stretch it, or even bounce it—there's so much to do with slime! But wait. We have questions. Is it a **liquid**? Is it a **solid**? It's certainly strange stuff!

!! NERD ALERT !!

Slime is a non-Newtonian fluid. This means that it doesn't act like other liquids, such as water or milk.

Look around you. Everything you can see is made up of some kind of material. Materials, such as wool, cardboard, glass, or plastic, are all different. They are good for different jobs because of their different **properties**.

SLIME IS A MATERIAL THAT HAS THE FOLLOWING PROPERTIES:

NOT QUITE SOLID

SQUEEZY

STRETCHY

FLOWS BUT ISN'T RUNNY

NOT QUITE LIQUID

THE SCIENCE OF SLIME

Many animals make their own natural slime. The parrotfish does something unusual with its slime, though. When some parrotfish go to sleep, they burp up a layer of clear, slimy **mucus** to sleep under!

MUCUS

!! NERD ALERT !!
The layer of slimy mucus may protect the parrotfish from <u>predators</u>.

WE CAN ALSO MAKE SLIME WITH SCIENCE!

Never touch chemicals without an adult!

When we mix two chemicals together, it can change their properties. By mixing the correct chemicals together, we can turn liquids, powders, and other things into slime!

LET'S TALK TEXTURE

Materials all feel different. Some are smooth, some are rough, some are soft, and some are bumpy. This is the texture of the material.

!! NERD ALERT !!
Can you find six materials in the room you are in that all have different textures?

METAL IS SMOOTH

FLUFF IS SOFT

TOY BRICKS ARE BUMPY

8

SAFETY FIRST!

THE GOLDEN RULES

1. Always make slime with a grown-up.

2. Don't swap in other ingredients because different reactions could happen.

3. DON'T EAT SLIME, and keep it away from your face.

!! NERD ALERT !!
If you are sensitive to any ingredients, wear long sleeves and gloves or use a different recipe.

TIME FOR SLIME

TO MAKE A BASIC WHITE SLIME YOU WILL NEED:

- ☐ 4 ounces (about 100 ml) of white school glue (PVA)

- ☐ Half a teaspoon of baking soda

- ☐ 1 teaspoon of contact lens solution

- ☐ Safety first!

DON'T FORGET!
Always make slime with a responsible adult!

Always make slime with a grown-up, and wear gloves and an apron while mixing.

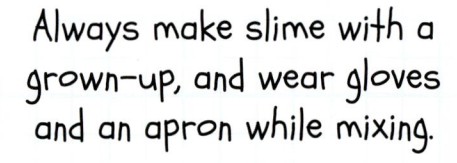

10

METHOD:

1. Put the glue in a bowl.

2. Add the baking soda and mix.

3. Add the contact lens solution and mix.

4. The slime will begin to form. It will look stringy at first so keep mixing! After about 30 seconds, the slime will form a ball.

11

MARVELOUS MIXING

Once you have made your basic slime, take a moment to **observe** it.

OBSERVATIONS

- What does it feel like?

- Does it stretch?

- Can I shape it?

- Does it bounce?

- Can I see through it?

You can change the texture of your slime by adding things to the mix.

WATER BEADS

GLITTER

FOAM BEADS

CONFETTI STARS

SAND

13

FOAM IT!

You can make your slime stiffer and more moldable by adding foam balls. Put your slime to one side, and make a second batch. This time, add in small foam balls when you add the contact lens solution.

You can add food coloring now too!

14

The more foam balls you mix in, the more the slime will hold its shape.

This type of slime is moldable, soft, and squishy. Because the foam balls thicken the slime, the slime can now be molded and shaped.

15

IS THAT CLEAR?

When you make slime with white glue, the slime will be thick. If you hold it up to the light, you won't be able to see much light passing through it. This means it is opaque.

OPAQUE SLIME

If you make slime with clear glue, light will pass through the slime. You will be able to see through it! This means it is transparent.

To make transparent slime, use the recipe for basic glue slime on pages 10 and 11. This time, use clear glue instead of white glue!

!! NERD ALERT !!
You will be able to see the things you mix into your slime more clearly if it is transparent.

GLITTER IT!

First, make a batch of clear slime. Stir in sparkly glitter and sequins before you add the contact lens solution.

Now make a batch of slime using white glue, with sequins and glitter. What do you notice about the two slimes?

!! NERD ALERT !!
To be scientific, make sure you add the same amount of glitter and sequins to each batch. You could use a spoon to measure it!

HOW ARE THEY DIFFERENT? HOW ARE THEY THE SAME?

MAKING A COMPARISON

Take a good look at your transparent slime and your opaque slime. Now see if you can answer these questions.

!! NERD ALERT !!
We're going to make a comparison. This means we are going to look at some things and notice what is different and what is the same about them.

Which one bounces highest?

Now compare your transparent slime and opaque slime with your foam slime. What can you observe? Do the slimes with foam and glitter act differently? Can you think of any questions of your own?

Which is the most sparkly?

Which one can stretch the farthest?

Which one will flow down a _slope_ the fastest?

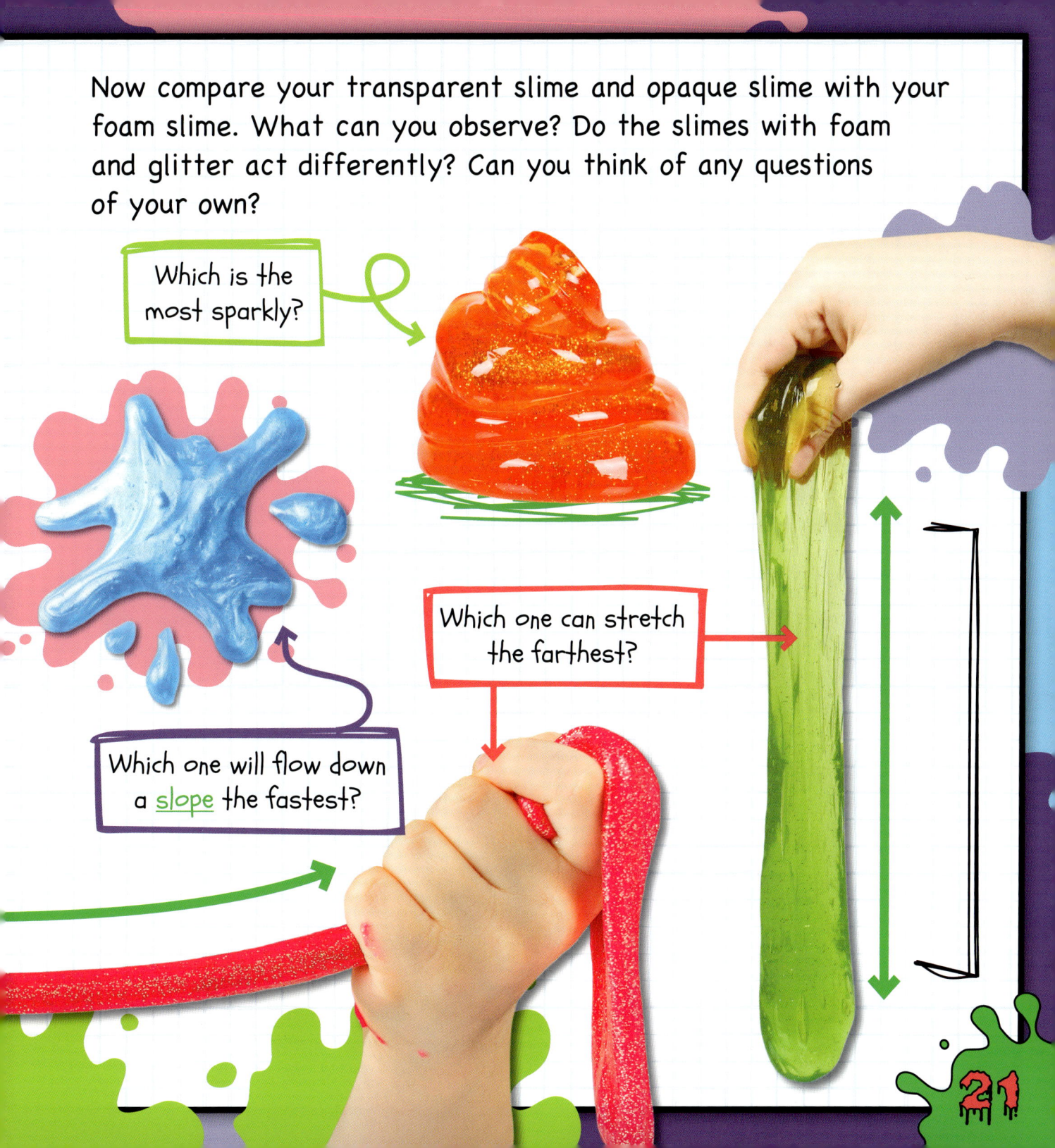

21

TIME TO EXPERIMENT

WHAT CAN YOU ADD TO YOUR SLIME TO CHANGE ITS PROPERTIES?

It's time to get creative. How can you change the texture of your slime, and what else can you find out?

QUESTIONS:

What can you add to make crunchy slime?

Can you blow a bubble into your slime using a straw? Which slime blows the best bubbles?

Which slime is the stickiest?

WHAT HAPPENS IF YOU ADD MORE THAN ONE THING?

GLOSSARY

CHEMICALS — matter that can cause changes when mixed with other matter

LIQUID — a material that flows, such as water

MEASURE — find out the exact size, weight, or amount of something

MUCUS — a slimy substance that helps protect and lubricate

OBSERVE — watch carefully to find something out

PREDATORS — animals that hunt other animals for food

PROPERTIES — features of something

REACTIONS — changes that happen when two or more things come into contact with each other

SENSITIVE — reacts strongly to something

SLOPE — a slant that goes up or down

SOLID — firm and stable, not a liquid

INDEX

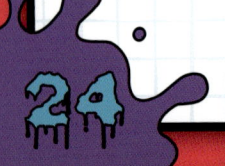